HODDER'S YEA
for the NATIONAL

A special introduction by William Mayne
for *Hodder's September Story Book*

THE
FOX GATE
AND OTHER STORIES

When I was young I used to run out of books to read. There used to be days when I had read everything in sight, especially the bits I didn't understand. Then I thought that if I wrote a book I could keep it in my toy box and read it whenever I wanted. The only trouble was, that the books I really liked had already been written. Also, I wasn't sure that just anyone was allowed to write a book. I mean, no one even had enough empty paper for that – it already had words on it – so perhaps I shouldn't try. But I did. Now I write books for me to read when I was young and it was raining and I wanted something I had never read before. The only trouble is, I already wrote it, and it isn't a surprise. But perhaps it's a rainy day for someone else, like you, and since you didn't write the book you might enjoy it.

A true story.

Hodder
Children's
Books

a division of Hodder Headline plc

Also by William Mayne

Captain Ming and the Mermaid

For older readers

Cradlefasts
Earthfasts
The Fairy Tales of London Town:
Upon Paul's Steeple
The Fairy Tales of London Town:
See-Saw Sacradown
A Swarm in May
Over the Hills and Far Away
Midnight Fair

THE
FOX GATE
AND OTHER STORIES

William Mayne

Illustrated by William Geldart

a division of Hodder Headline plc

Text copyright © 1996 William Mayne
Illustrations copyright © 1996 William Geldart

First published in Great Britain in 1996
by Hodder Children's Books

This edition published in Great Britain in 1999
by Hodder Children's Books

The right of William Mayne to be identified as the Author of
the Work has been asserted by him in accordance with the
Copyright, Designs and Patents Act 1988.

10 9 8 7 6 5 4 3 2 1

All rights reserved. No part of this publication may be
reproduced, stored in a retrieval system, or transmitted,
in any form or by any means without the prior written
permission of the publisher, nor be otherwise circulated
in any form of binding or cover other than that in which
it is published and without a similar condition being
imposed on the subsequent purchaser.

All characters in this publication are fictitious and any resemblance
to real persons, living or dead, is purely coincidental.

A Catalogue record for this book is available from the British Library

ISBN 0340 75282 3

Printed and bound in Great Britain by
The Guernsey Press Co. Ltd, Guernsey, Channel Islands

Hodder Children's Books
A Division of Hodder Headline plc
338 Euston Road
London NW1 3BH

CONTENTS

Madrina	9
Jack and Jill	23
A Twisty Path	37
The Fox Gate	51
The Smallest Present	63
The Jewel	73
The Foxer	79

For Ariel Baker-Gibbs

Madrina

Gwazir is used to walking across the desert, and every day or so there is a tree, and water to drink. With him are five mules, who are looking after him, and three camels, looking after three men. That is what Gwazir thinks. The men are looking after the camels, and Gwazir is looking after the mules, but it is hard to tell Gwazir about it, because he is quite deaf, except for one thing.

"Ho, hay," say the men, "he does his work; what does it matter what he thinks?"

Gwazir does not hear what they say. He does not know why they open their mouths when there is nothing to eat, but he knows that men and camels always say something cross.

Gwazir understands the mules' mouths much better.

The grandmother mule is the leader, and called Madrina. She has blue beads round her long ears, and very wise eyes. She can kick with her back legs harder than anything else in the world. Even the camels stay away, and the men will not come near. Only Gwazir can walk behind her, because they trust each other.

Gwazir knows she is looking after him, because he can hear her. Round her neck she has a bell, and when she rings it he can hear a sharp, high noise, like a bird at the top of the sky. Then he knows she is telling him something.

Nothing else in the world makes any sound for him.

The men, and the camels, and the mules, and Gwazir, walk across the burning sand, and among the blazing rocks.

They start before the sun gets up.

They stop when the sun treads hottest on them. The men brew tea and drink it very sweet. The camels look disagreeable, hiccup horribly, and chew the cud.

Madrina leads the four other mules away to find something to eat among the dry rocks. Gwazir goes with them.

"That boy looks after the mules well," say the men. "He does not spend his time idly gossiping."

This day Madrina and the others

wander among the rocks. Gwazir sits in the shade of one. The lizards and the scorpions come out to look at him.

Gwazir thinks they are crossing the desert too, going to the town, like him. The town has plenty to eat, shady buildings, many trees, and water if you ask for it.

Out in the dry desert, sunshine is nearly all the weather. Today the camels are very uneasy. They call and grunt to each other, and tell the men. But the men only shout at them.

Among the rocks as big as houses Madrina rings her bell. Gwazir comes to her.

"What is it?" he asks her, but he says it with his eyes and with his hands. "What is the matter?"

Madrina shakes her head, and rings the bell again. The other mules come to her, and she leads them where she thinks it is best. Gwazir follows, because she is in charge.

She takes them into a dry valley with high sides like the cliffs, and tells them to wait. Something is coming.

The camels make so much noise the men wake up and want to hit them with sticks. When they stand up they see what is the matter.

The day is hotter than ever, but there is no sunshine. The sky has grown dark, but not with night. It has turned brown with flying sand. A sandstorm is coming on a gale of wind.

The men pack up all their goods, the kettle and their beds and food. They shout for Gwazir, but he hears nothing. They yell for Madrina, but she is a mile away. Even if she hears, she is too sensible to move from where she is.

"What is the use of a deaf boy?" say the men. "We shall lose all the mules and everything they are carrying."

And the boy too, think the camels. There are altogether too many boys, to beat the camels with sticks every day. Now, say the camels, heads down, noses shut, and eyes closed. That's the way to have a sandstorm.

The men drop their skin tents down and lie under them.

Gwazir sees the sky turn brown and knows what is coming.

Madrina puts her wise head to the cliff of the valley, and waits.

"It is the blue beads," thinks Gwazir. "They bring wisdom."

But the other mules are not wise.

They run into the desert and Gwazir can do nothing about it. The sandstorm comes like a fiery blizzard that fills his face and stings his chest inside. He puts his head to the cliff and tries to breathe.

The camels go on chewing, and
the sand drifts against them. They see
all their footprints fill in and the skins of
the tents begin to turn sandy.

Then it is too dark to see anything.
The wind blows so strong and fierce
that the camels decide it is night and go
to sleep. Madrina and Gwazir, in their
sheltered valley, wriggle their shoulders
because hot sand heaps on their backs.

Gwazir breathes through a corner
of his shirt, and the air is like an oven.
His eyes fill with sand, and it gets
between his teeth and down his throat.

After a long time, the sand stops
falling, but the day is no brighter
because night is nearly here now.
Madrina knows the way back to camp.

But first the four lost mules have to
be found.

"We shall have to do it," says
Gwazir, and Madrina rings her bell.

Perhaps it is reply, or maybe she is calling the other mules. But they do not come.

Gwazir climbs on Madrina's back, and Madrina rings her bell again. The driving sand has made it shiny on the side. They do not know which way to go because the ground is new and nobody has walked on it before.

They go into the gathering darkness, climbing on the rocks, looking into the dusk, trying to see the four lost mules. Footprints begin to show in the drifted sand, not clear at first, but growing sharper and deeper.

All at once night is complete all over the desert. Footprints can no longer be seen. Madrina stops walking. Gwazir climbs down from her back, and tries to feel the track on the ground under the cold stars. His mouth is full of sand and he longs for water.

The moon grows into the sky like a slice of water-melon. Gwazir feels more thirsty, but the ground shows again. On it now are other prints that are not those of a mule, but of some hunting animal that came this way.

Madrina looks round. Gwazir looks round too, for hunting animals that might hunt mules. There are shadows in the desert now, and some of them seem to move.

Gwazir thinks he sees the mules far away, sand-blown and unhappy, standing together, frightened and lonely. Madrina rings her bell. Gwazir climbs on her back again, and they go to find them.

There is a noise. Gwazir cannot hear it, but Madrina can, and so can the other mules. They stamp and twitch. Madrina turns her head.

"What is the matter?" asks Gwazir, with his heart and hands.

"Look," says Madrina, and he looks.

Behind them is a desert lion. In the moonlight it is the same colour as the sand. It has seen Madrina.

Gwazir kicks her side, but Madrina does not move. She shakes her head and rings her bell.

The lion hears that. It walks, then hurries a little, then bounds, and leaps, and hurls himself forward, straight at Madrina.

Gwazir wants to shout, and does not know how. He wants to get off Madrina's back, but he cannot move.

The lion is in the air, and the shadow flies across the ground. But there is something he does not know about Madrina.

It is not the bell. It is not the blue beads. Madrina knows about it. It is her kick. She waits quietly with the kick all ready.

The Fox Gate

When the lion's leap is nearly on her back, his claws coming out to grip her, his teeth ready to tear at Gwazir, she lets it go.

She kicks herself out to her own length again. Madrina got to the lion before the lion got to Madrina. The lion rolls over and over in the moonlight,

Madrina

with a great hurt howl. Then it creeps away, not hungry for mules any more.

Gwazir gets down from Madrina's back. She is quite calm now. She knew what her duty was, and did it. But Gwazir has ridden on top of her kick, and it went all through him. His legs feel very strange and trembly.

The other mules are glad to be found. Gwazir ties them in a long line, and Madrina leads them all back to the camp.

The camels are deep in sand and too comfortable to get up. They mean to stay here all night and listen to Madrina's story, and tell the men, because Gwazir cannot.

The men are deaf to that, but are pleased the mules are safe.

"Ho hay, well done," they say, and give Gwazir tea and bread, and blue beads of his own round his neck.

When Madrina tells what happened Gwazir hears only her bell high in the moon.

And the sandy lion is still limping across the desert.

Jack and Jill

Jack and Jill and the rest of the jackdaws live in the fields all winter. If there is a fine day most of them look down chimneys for a nesting place.

But Jack and Jill do not need to. They know their nest. It is high up in the end of a stone barn, above the fifth row of the binding stones that jut out and hold the wall together.

Inside the barn the calves spend

the snowy time, eating and drinking. Their breath is all steam in the cold air.

Inside the walls, wood mice spend their time eating hay.

Trixie, the chintz cat from the farm, comes day after day to look about. She listens for mice.

"Hush," she says to the calves, when they speak to her. She sits on a post among them and waits for a mouse to come out.

The snow melts away and all the world outside is green. The sky turns warmer, and Jack and Jill come back. Trixie sits outside, watching for mice and now and then chattering her teeth at Jack or Jill.

Other jackdaws take a look at the nest, so there are sudden squabbles and shouts. Jill wonders whether it is good enough.

"Quick, quick," says Jack, showing

it to her, hoping she remembers what a good house it is.

So she hops in at last, and looks round. "Of course," she says. "This is home. You are so silly, dear."

They are not the only ones thinking about a nest. Trixie is looking in a corner of the hay, inside the barn.

"You know it is," says Trixie to Jill. "It's family time."

"Cats don't lay eggs," says Jill to Jack. "Do they?"

"Not usually," says Jack, and thinks about the matter.

Soon there are five eggs, outside and high up. Inside and low down there are five kittens. The calves can't tell which is which, because all small young things sound the same.

Trixie purrs and the kittens drink milk. The little jackdaws eat things that are still wriggling. They like that best.

Baby jackdaws begin to grow feathers. Kittens open their eyes.

The biggest kitten is called Tiger. He goes out of the barn into the sunshine and jumps on the grass. He jumps after a fly going by. He jumps up on the first row of sticking-out stones.

"Come back, come back," call the others, looking up at him. They think it is very high. So does Tiger.

Jill flies overhead to her nest, carrying a great big grub who had meant to be a beetle. She sees the kittens.

"Too big to eat," she says, wondering what colour their egg shells were.

Trixie brings the kittens their first mouse. They don't know they have to eat it, and it gets away.

A few days later Tiger climbs up on the first row of stones again, and jumps down on his brothers and sisters. They have biting and scratching fun, until Trixie calls them in.

The next day they all get up on the stones, and jump off, and fall off, and can't remember how to get down.

The next day after that Tiger climbs up on the next row. This must be the top, he thinks.

"They're getting nearer," says Jack, flying in. "Have you invited them, Jill?"

"No," says Jill. "They won't get any higher, will they?"

"I hope not," says Jack.

Tiger has got to be rescued by Trixie, because in the end he is frightened of the ground, so very far away.

But a day or two later he is up on the second row again, marching along from end to end. He chatters his teeth at the other kittens, and is so surprised that he falls off.

The Fox Gate

"I don't think we need worry," says Jack.

"If you're sure," says Jill.

"Am I ever wrong?" says Jack.

The next day there are five kittens on the second row of stones. But Trixie won't go up for them. They have to come down to her.

"We shall never go up there again," say four of them. And the fifth one says, "I shall go higher still," and he chatters his teeth at the moon.

Jack says, "I still think we needn't worry, dear."

Jill worries, but doesn't say anything. She tries to forget that cats eats birds, and that five kittens could eat five little jackdaws just like that.

The next day there is a big upset and turmoil. The farmer comes to take the calves out into a field. He opens the door and sends them all out into the open air and down behind the barn.

Trixie and the kittens rush outside too, or they will be trodden underfoot.

"Come up on the first row," says Trixie, because the calves are coming along the end of the building.

Then she takes them up to the second row. But the calves are so big now that Trixie takes the kittens to the third row and makes them sit in a line.

Jack coming homewards with a mouse, is so alarmed to see the kittens so high up that he drops the mouse instead of giving it to his nestlings. Tiger gets it, and makes a tremendous fuss of eating it.

All the other kittens look up towards the jackdaws' nest and ask for their own.

Then the calves have gone, and the kittens climb down, and Jill comes home.

Jack is walking up and down on the roof worrying very much. "What shall we do?" he says.

"I don't know, dear," says Jill. "But it's always meal time in the nest, so worry while you work."

Tiger fell off twice a day for the next week, but on Sunday he was up on the fourth row. On Monday two more kittens are there with him, on Tuesday three, and on Wednesday there are four.

"Come down," says Trixie, but by now the kittens are getting too old to obey her except when she is very close or very cross.

At last they come down, but Trixie has gone off on her own so there is nothing to eat. All the kittens have to jump on is the waving grass, and they bite its neck and growl, but they can't eat it.

The calves think it's lovely, but

there, tastes differ.

Trixie comes back for the night. But the nest is not quite big enough any more, and there is not enough milk. And Trixie goes away before breakfast.

"We've got to look after ourselves," say the kittens.

"Yes," says Tiger. "Me first."

And they hunt for mice along the bottom of the wall. But the mice stay inside the wall, eating hay.

One kitten kills a dandelion. A thistle bites another.

Tiger goes up on the first row of stones.

"Nothing to worry about," says Jack, worrying quite a lot in case he is wrong. Jackdaws have grey hair from that, anyway.

Tiger climbs to the second row. There is something higher up, he knows. Something that moves about.

You can eat things that move about and are difficult to catch.

Another kitten follows him to the first row, and to the second. By the time Tiger is on the third row there are three kittens climbing the wall.

"They're definitely on the way," says Jack.

"I know," says Jill "But you would have this nest."

"Quick, quick," says Jack, but they don't know what to do.

Tiger is on the fourth row, looking for the fifth. Jack thinks of giving him a peck, but Tiger stands up and fights back.

"We're coming," say his brothers and sisters.

"Me first," says Tiger, reaching up for the fifth row. It isn't easy, but he knows he can do it. And he can hear that there is a nestful just up there.

Jack and Jill come down to the barn. They walk about on the roof. They walk about on the fifth row of stones. They look down at Tiger.

Their little ones come and look out too, and ask what the matter is. In all the fuss and noise one of them falls out of the nest.

"Look out," calls Jill, and goes to help. But the young jackdaw opens out its wings and helps itself. It flies around and lands on the roof.

"Of course," says Jack, "that's what they do. They fly. I quite forgot."

And one by one the young jackdaws swoop out over Tiger's head.

He does not see. When he climbs to the fifth row there is no one there. The nest is warm, but empty. He sits down to have a rest.

And Jack, coming with a furry caterpillar for a young jackdaw, forgets that they have left the nest, and lands in front of it. Tiger hisses, like a young jackdaw with his mouth open. Jack puts the caterpillar in. A mouth is a mouth after all.

Tiger climbs down, spitting and coughing. Trixie comes back and leads them all away. Jackdaws fly off laughing, and the barn is empty except for mice. The caterpillar crawls home.

A Twisty Path

In the long grass beside the big patch of concrete there lived a snail called Levi.

He thought the big patch of concrete might be a road, and there would be somewhere else at the other side. He could not see very far, only about his own length, but there was always something at the end of it.

"I haven't reached the end yet. I'll

keep it in mind," he said.

He pinned a little note up inside his shell, and took another snail's pace through the grass, saying hello to friends like Mr Helix. There was always time for a meal between words.

Now, it was springtime, and moontime, and warm rain time, and the grass was rich and fresh, and, "I should be happy," said Levi to himself.

He ate a green leaf right down to the ground, stalk and all, and it was tender and sweet, but it wasn't what would make him happy.

"Perhaps I need a change," he thought. "I wonder about going to the other side of the concrete." But it was very far across, and he was sure he didn't know the way.

"What if that's not the going-across way, but the going-along way?" he wondered. "I'd never get anywhere."

He didn't actually know about places. Snails don't ever move house, so they don't think about places. They just change gardens.

Still, Levi wasn't quite happy. But he went on eating between words, even when it rained on his picnic.

When the sun came out he curled up in his shell and waited until things were more comfortable.

Sometimes there was something much louder than sunshine, and much nearer. Old Mr Helix, who had the biggest shell of all, said it was lightning.

And sometimes there was a much worse thing, ever so near, and with ever so much smoke and the ground shaking. No one knew what it was, except Levi. "It's frightening," he said. "That's what it is."

"Earthquake," said Mr Helix.

But they hadn't had that for a long time.

One day, when the sun had gone away, Levi came out and saw what he really needed.

There was the prettiest girl snail anyone could ever hope to see, and she was looking at him. She was looking at him in quite a friendly way. She looked at him as if she might like him, Levi thought.

She had eyes of blue on a very elegant stalks. She had a very attractive striped shell. She smiled and showed a charming set of teeth.

Levi fell in love at once. "That's why I'm unhappy," he said to himself. "No one loves me."

"I wonder if it's true," said the girl snail. Her name was Dextry.

They looked at one another. Levi asked whether he could buy her a blade of grass, and she said, "Have one of mine," and they both felt a bit shy.

"But I think it'll be all right," said Levi to himself. "She does like me."

Then Dextry's smile wasn't quite so charming, and her eyes looked at him in a funny way.

"I'm afraid I have to go now," she said, in a sad but certain manner. "I'm afraid we can't be friends."

"But why?" asked Levi. "What is wrong?"

"Simple, I'm afraid," said Dextry. "My shell twists one way, and yours twists the other, and there's nothing we can do about it."

"Shell?" said Levi, "Twists?" And he looked. And she was right. Her shell went one way from the middle, right-handed, and his went the other way, left-handed.

And off Dextry went, quite slowly. but quite for ever. And Levi stood where he hoped a bird would eat him. His heart was broken. He did not care whether his shell cracked too.

"Is there a problem?" asked old Mr Helix, coming by. His shell was right-handed from the middle too.

"That proves it," said Levi. "There is something wrong with me. What shall I do?"

But the sun was coming out and Mr Helix closed his shell and went to sleep.

"I shall leave forever," said Levi. "But it doesn't feel like Levi for ever."

In the night he crawled up on the

concrete and set out through the darkness. "Perhaps I'll reach the edge of the world," he said, "and that'll be that."

Well, he was right and he was wrong. He went on until he bumped into something standing there, and climbed up that instead, because it was smooth and easy and cool.

Daylight came, and he found he was up a tower. At least, down was further down than he could see, and up was further up and so were the sides. And it was all white and shining.

He went walking, up and up. "The top will be better," he said, and on he sorrowfully went, weeping a snaily tear now and then from the tips of his eyes, when he thought of Dextry.

Far away down below Dextry was just as unhappy. "But I can't marry a left-twisted snail," she said to herself.

"Even if he asks me."

Up on his white tower Levi felt the sun come out. He became very uncomfortable. Tears dried up. His foot began to get hard. His eyes folded right back. He tried to climb into a crack, but it was too small.

Then, all at once, the crack opened up. and there was a shadow.

Levi crept through the doorway in the side of a space rocket on its launch pad, while the men set it ready to fire. The men closed the door and went away. Levi was left alone.

Levi climbed up on the flight deck. Levi climbed up on the Control Panel. Levi had a bit of a twirl on the knobs. Levi crawled over the notice that said IGNITION. He thought it just said "Lumpy", because it was. He crawled on to the switch.

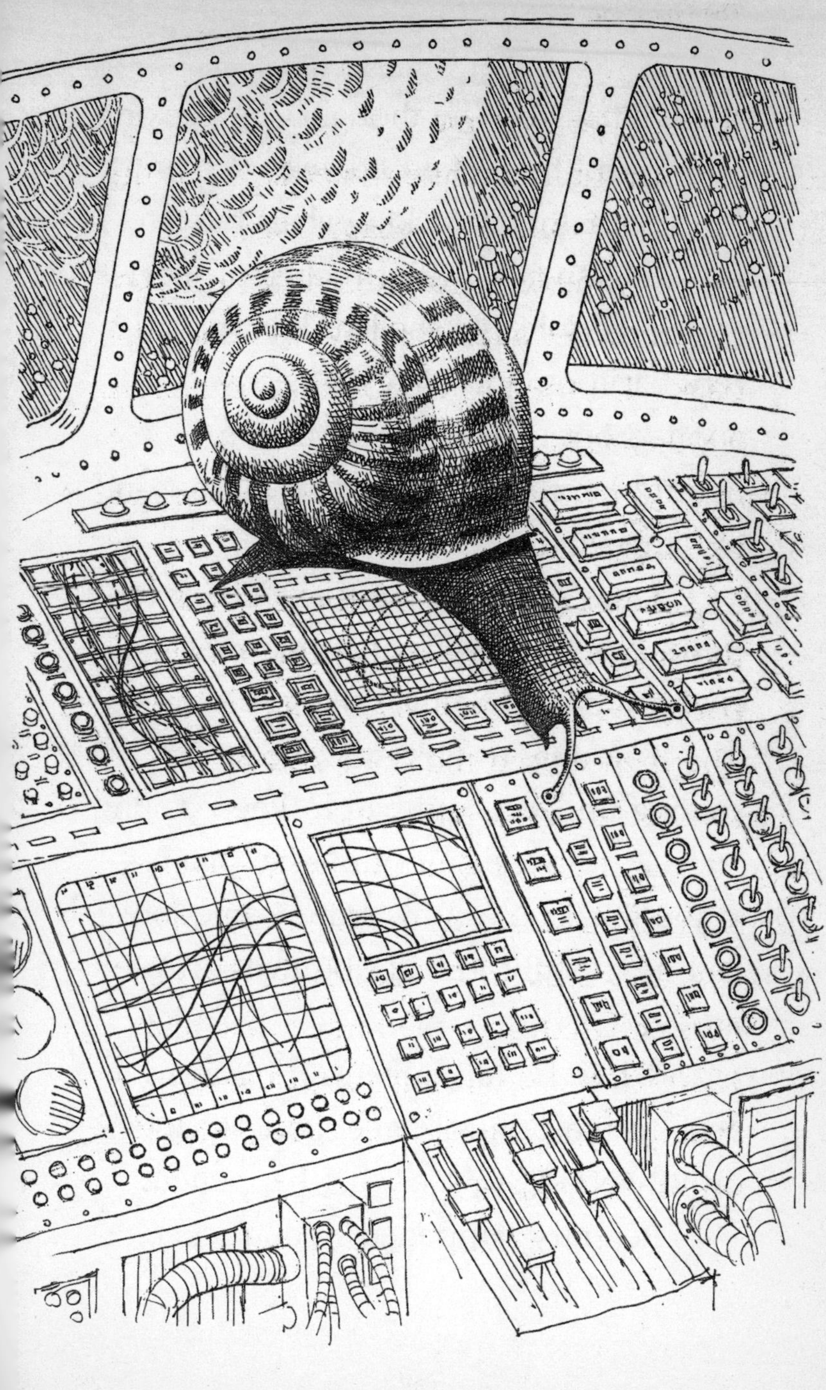

"What fun," he thought. "A rocking chair." And he rocked it back.

It was not a rocking chair but a rocketing switch, and it rocketed. Levi grew a very heavy shell suddenly, and a very flat foot, and his eyes nearly popped out of his head. Mission Control kept shouting to him but not in his language.

All at once he was weightless. He could run, even with only one foot. He could turn somersaults. He could fly.

The only trouble was, he kept coming undone, and had to keep coiling himself up because of the draughtiness in the joints. Even his name came loose and he thought it might be Evil, or Live, or Elvi.

When he felt tidy again he went back to the Control Panel and sat down on RE-ENTRY, to see what happened.

Re-entry happened. The rocket

came back to earth. It grew hot, and dizzy, and the right way up, and landed back on its launch pad.

Levi ended up in the corner by the door, hoping his shell was not cracked. When the man came rushing back to see what had gone wrong he rolled out and tumbled to the ground. He landed in the grass, not on the concrete, and went to look for a leaf to eat and shelter under. There was no grass in space.

"Did you find anything interesting?" asked Mr Helix.

"I'm an astrosnail," said Levi. "It was out of this world."

"So I've heard," said Mr Helix. "You missed the earthquake, and there's a friend of yours coming, so I'll be off," And in half a day he was.

And in the same half day Dextry came near him again.

"I wish she wouldn't," said Levi to

himself. "My heart is broken. But that's love."

"I'm so sorry," she said. "I really did admire you, and if it wasn't just for one thing, we could be such friends."

"Oh well," said Levi, "that's the way it is," and it was like a dart through his heart.

"Wait a minute," said Dextry. "You've changed. You really have. What have you done?"

"Nothing," said Levi. "Please don't make it worse."

"But you are the right way round now," said Dextry. "We are both the same, and everything will be all right."

"Am I?" said Levi. And he looked. And he was. Somewhere in weightlessness, when he came loose, he had put himself together the other way about, and now they were both the same. Her shell went from the middle, right-handed, and now Levi's went from the middle, right-handed, too. "Yes," he said. "I am." He was very surprised, but kept his wits about him. "I did it for you," he said. "Of course."

"Of course," she said. "Now tell me your name."

"Ivel," said Levi. Because that had been put the other way round too. "My name is Ivel."

So they lived happily and right-handedly ever afterwards. The children were right-handed, left-handed, and twins.

The Fox Gate

From the high walls of the city the soldiers watch the sunny day. Through the city gates farmers' carts slowly go, or swiftly runs the proud carriage of the prince. Outside the walls thirsty cows eat withered grass on the slope. The city ditch is dry.

Men are thirsty too, and wish for rain. The prince proclaims that prayers must be said by all citizens that night in the cathedral.

At his door sits Fox. It is no grand gate like those of men, but a rough hole among the great stones at the foot of the wall. Vixen and the cubs sleep.

They do not speak with voices in the day, but understand each lift of the ear and turn of the eye, each paw's movement and the swing of brush.

Only Fox sees with huntsman's eye a gathering of men beyond the city ditch, at the forest edge secretly. From turret and battlement the city soldiers do not see.

"What men do is nothing to me," says Fox. He waits for night and the clear moon of summer. "They have their gates and goings and I have mine, and our ways are not the same."

But Fox is wrong. Men are to follow his ways before the moon is high.

At dusk the great cathedral bells

call all men to prayer. City gates are closed and bolted firm. The streets are dark, but safe, the people think. A thousand candles light the cathedral windows.

The moon is low in the trees of the forest. Under it stir the feet and swords of the city's enemies.

"It is nothing to me," says Fox. "All men are enemies."

"It is quiet in the city tonight," says Vixen. "But in the forest there is movement. We shall catch nothing there."

"I shall hunt the city rats and look in larders," says Fox. He has a way into the city through the wall into the palace garden.

There he hears the cathedral sing. "How men howl," he thinks. Along the street alone he runs in a shadow to the square. He licks the water pump and tastes only rust. All is dry still. Beside the baker's shop he finds a mouldered loaf to take home. He goes back to the palace garden down among the stones, with the moonlight following him.

Then his hackles rise and his fur stands stiff. He hears sounds he always dreaded. Men are at his dwelling, breaking out the blocks of stone.

Vixen and the cubs crawl fearful up to him. "Go further," he says, "and stay in the garden."

Fox lays down the mouldered loaf and goes to see what men these are, and why they come. They are men from the forest, who have spied his hole at the foot of the wall, and are breaking in with spears, swords and axes, while the city folk pray.

Stones are hauled aside, rubble taken away. A hole man-high is being made, as quiet as it can.

The Fox Gate

Fox watches. These men care nothing for what he does; they are not looking for him, Vixen, or the cubs. Tonight they are hunting a city.

Fox comes to the garden again. His home has gone, thrown down the slope, and men are coming through.

"What we can do I cannot tell," says Fox to Vixen. "If we stay here perhaps they will not notice us."

"I think," says Vixen, "that we should pray too, with the city folk." Perhaps she has read the proclamation and knows where the people are. "They are our own people, we must trust them."

At the cathedral the choristers' door is open. Inside, the people pray for prince and peace. Between their words the foxes pad along an aisle like a stone forest. A thousand candle flames stand in every foxy eye.

The foxes move among the feet of all the people, who stand to sing an anthem. Wax drips like warm ice. To the front they come, with the organ piping like birds in high branches of the vault.

"Vixen," says Fox, "what is praying?" He comes out from among the people. He goes to tell the man carrying a shepherd's crook, who may understand. It is the bishop at his altar.

Before he comes to the bishop a chorister sees him and points, and then all the other boys. The singing stops. Vixen is glad of that. But all eyes, glittering with flame and amazement, now look at Fox. Fox licks his lips dry. He cannot speak, and if he did, who would understand?

He is ready to escape, but does not know where to go, all alone in a great paved place. He sees shadows and runs for them, up some steps, and at the top he can go no further. He stands where preachers stand; but Fox has no sermon today.

The man with the hat and crook has turned to see why all the music broke and died. He stretches out his hand and makes the people calm.

"All God's creatures pray today," he says. "No harm must come to any."

Down he kneels in his own church and picks a fox cub up. Vixen takes his silken sleeve and pulls. She is not afraid.

"Come down," she says to Fox. "And lead to where the forest men break in."

"Follow me," says Fox, with voice, and twitch of ear, turn of eye, point of foot and swing of brush.

"Come," says Vixen, as if to a cub, and brings the bishop along. He understands. She drops his sleeve so he may walk. She runs to Fox and back to bishop, and they go through the boy's door into the street.

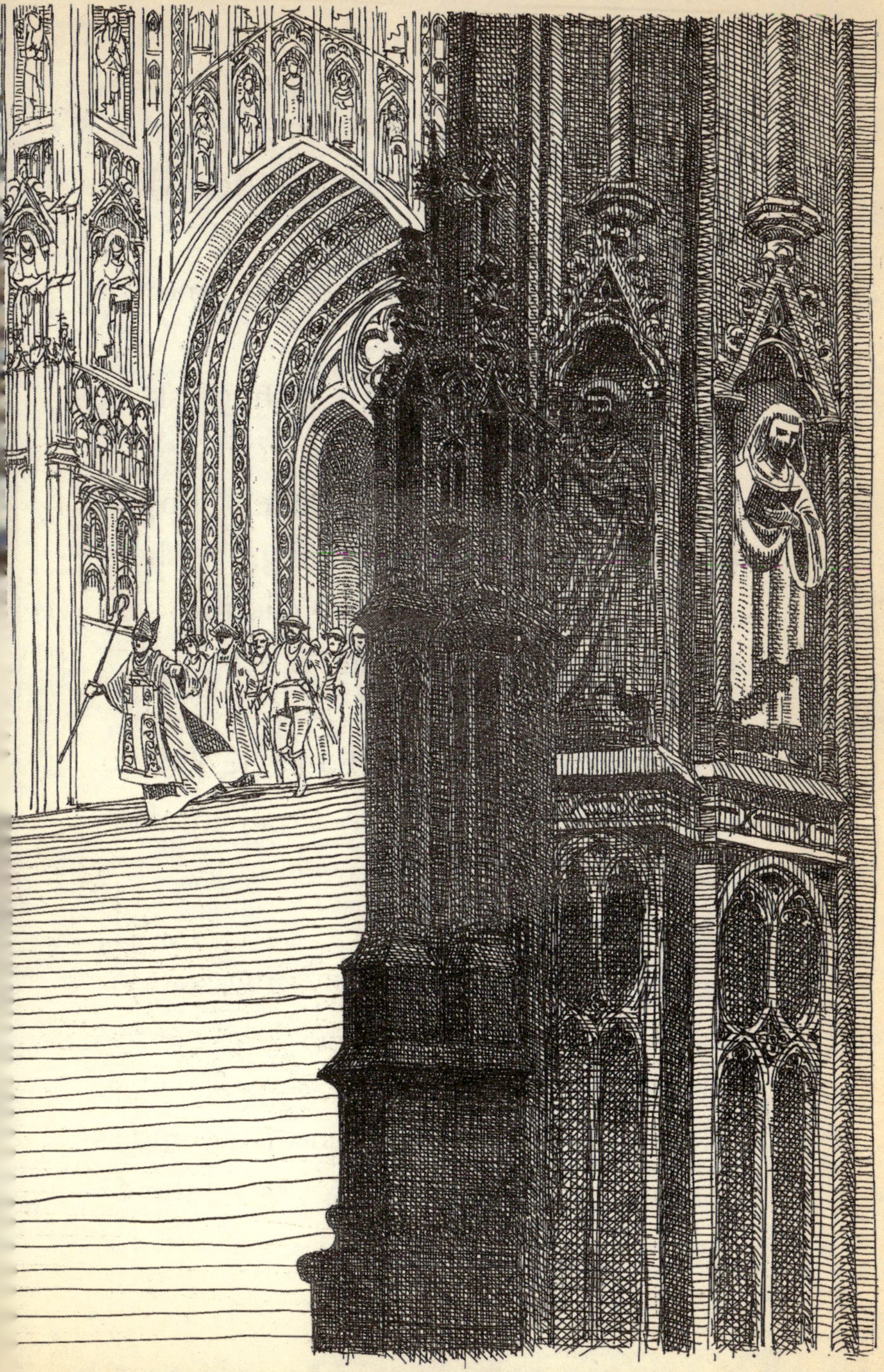

Behind the bishop comes the choir, then the priests, the soldiers, and last of all the prince. He hurries forward when the palace gate is reached.

Fox goes to his secret way, and pauses at the hole.

"What is below?" the bishop asks, "what do I hear dig, and why?"

The prince and his soldiers slip out their swords, and the moonlight flashes on the steel. They put the choirboys up the wall to look down the other side and shout and point.

And that is that. The forest men run down the bank, across the city ditch and are lost among the trees. City soldiers find none at all.

The bishop takes his congregation to the cathedral, prince, choristers and foxes, and they finish the prayers. At their last amen a high cloud is behind the moon, and before day comes there is rain.

The city wall is next day mended, and the archway made, a door for the Fox and family, called The Fox Gate, with its name above it.

The prince lays the centre stone.

"They saved the city; we must honour them," he says, and the bishop blesses it.

The Smallest Present

A mouse called Befana lived in a corner of the palace, until he fell into the pit under the floor, where the rye was kept. The lid was put on and he could not get out.

So he lived there instead, eating as much as he liked. "I'm living like the king," he thought.

Every day rye would be scooped up for the king's bread, and every day Befana saw light come in as the lid was lifted, and he kept out of the way of the scoop.

But one night there was a noise above him in the darkness. People were walking about, talking, and packing up goods and luggage. Befana did not hear the lid being lifted, and no light came in because it was night.

He was caught in the scoop along with the rye and put in a bag, with more rye being put on him until the bag was full.

He had to swim up to the top of the bag, sneezing in the dust. Before he could get out, the neck of the bag was tied, and that was that. It was a leather bag, but hard as iron.

He heard the king talking. He heard two kings talking. He heard three kings talking.

"Too many," he said to himself.

"Too many," said another voice.

It was the palace camel. "Too many kings, and the night's too dark, and I don't fancy that bright star in the sky. I don't like changes, that's what."

"Nor do I," said Befana. "Where are you going?"

"Round the moon, I daresay," said the camel. "I shan't enjoy it, I never do."

"Tell me about it when you come back," said Befana.

"If I get back," said the camel, "it will be too painful to remember. That's what it's like being a camel."

Then the camel stood up, because the king told him to. Befana banged his head on the hard leather bag, dusty again when the grains of rye had flown about.

"Good-bye," said the camel. "Probably for ever." And he began to plod along following the star.

Each plod of each foot shook Befana again. He realised that the bag had been strapped to the saddle, and that he and the rye were luggage, going along on the journey through the night.

"Camel go softly," he said. "My head aches."

"If it's good enough for the king it's better than you deserve," said the camel. "I don't know why you aren't walking. Or carrying me. You enjoy scuttling about."

But, "Oh," thought Befana, "I don't enjoy being banged about in this bag, and all the dust."

Night was so cold, and the day was so hot; and all the time the kings talked about the long journey ahead.

"We camels do the work," said the camel, "the kings sit there; and that mouse is the last straw."

After many days Befana's bag was

taken from the saddle and opened. A king's hand came in and took out a handful of rye. Another king was to grind it into flour, and the third king would cook it over a fire.

Befana scrambled out of the bag without being seen and ran to hide under the saddle.

"Stop tickling," said the camel. "I can't abide itches."

"It's me," said Befana. "Where are we? All I can see is the desert."

"It's all there is," said the camel. "We're lost. The star doesn't get any nearer. It's going round in circles."

But the kings were happy about their journey. They were getting near their destination.

"Just taking presents to someone," said the camel. "Why they can't stick a stamp on like anyone else I don't know."

The king looked at the presents, to see that they were travelling well. There was a golden jar, twinkling in starlight there was a bundle of twigs and leaves with a sad smell, and there was a packet with a rich and lovely scent.

"Nothing you could eat," said the camel. "Nothing useful."

Before the bag of rye was tied up again Befana went into it and brought out enough grains for a day or two and hid them in the folds of the saddle cloth.

"Thank you for reminding me," he

said to the camel.

"Don't thank me," said the camel. "I'm just walking."

Befana could see where he was going now, and that the star was coming closer to the ground. They went on through the desert until there were towns ahead, and there the kings asked the way.

"I knew we were lost," said the camel.

At last the star stood over a village a long way off. Befana was glad, because he had used up all the rye he had hidden, and the bag was empty. The kings were hungry too. Only the camel had eaten some good thorns. There were better ones at home, he said.

They came to a stable, and went in.

The first king gave his present to a little baby boy, who had to lie in a manger on some straw. The present was the gold, which kings give to kings. The second and the third king gave theirs too, and the baby understood and looked at them.

"Camels don't give presents," said the camel. "I never heard of it, anyway, so mine's a rotten one." He gave his last bundle of thorns. "All I had," he said. "It'll make a fire, or something. Now come on, what about you, mouse?"

Befana had nothing to give at all. He had eaten all the rye. So he hid in a fold of the saddle cloth. And out of another fold fell one grain of rye, the very last of all the bag.

He gave that, and was ashamed of giving such a small thing. He would rather have given nothing.

"If you drop it on to the ground," he said to the baby, "it grows up into a plant with more rye on it. But mice forget that, and men do it for them."

The baby smiled at him for the smallest present, and gave him a crust of bread dipped in wine, so that he felt warm and sleepy, not ashamed any more.

"Now we just go home," said the camel. "There and back, plod, plod,

plod, that's a camel's life. I knew it would all be to do again.

"Stop grumbling," said Befana. "I'm sleepy."

"I only grumble when I'm happy," said the camel. "I'm only happy when I grumble."

But Befana was asleep. Three kings, their journey over, nodded in their saddles. And, its work finished, the star had set behind the hills of Galilee.

The Jewel

Buff, a toad under the grass with his heels out and his thumbs in, caught Black Fly.

"Knees in, wings back, please," said Buff to Black Fly, trapped on his long tongue.

"Buzz," said Black Fly. It had not happened to him before; he did not wish it now. Buff swallowed him. Black Fly did not fold his wings or bend his legs. Maggots are not raised civil

The Fox Gate

any more, thought Buff, and I've not felt well all day.

Striped Fly came by, Homberson Bomberson. "Don't catch me, I sting," he buzzed, stripy, noisy, hot in the sun.

Buff lived in a little garden, where a cottage stood. The garden was quite bare. All that could go into the pot had been eaten now. There was no shelter. Homberson Bomberson hung over his head and buzzed. For Buff it was too hot. He had a mortal headache now.

He crawled through the cottage doorway and sat on the cold stone. He was poorly, but the people were in poverty; the woman and her children licked their fingers to live.

The sun set. Children lay down hungry. Buff spread his elbows and put his hand on his aching head.

The woman of the cottage said, "You'd better be outside; no one has

The Jewel

food here," and lifted him out to the cool dark.

Buff lay there all night, his head large and larger with pain. In the morning Homberson Bomberson came to buzz.

Buff crept to the shade of the kitchen corner. Sadness was in the cottage, the people were in sorrow.

"Today's joy," they said, "is that we're poorer still tomorrow."

At night they led Buff outside. What can tomorrow bring? he thought. Nothing eats us toads. We live in vain.

By morning he was too weak to move. The kind but starving people put him in the darkest corner of the house and poured cold water on his pained head, all they had.

Homberson Bomberson cried, "Come and join the fun."

Buff, with his hand on his ears,

wondered how he could take his aching head right off, like some hat. All afternoon he pulled and pushed. As the sun began to set he felt his skull begin to move. As shadows fell the joint above his mouth grew loose. As darkness came around, hard thing dropped on his tongue, and all his pain was over.

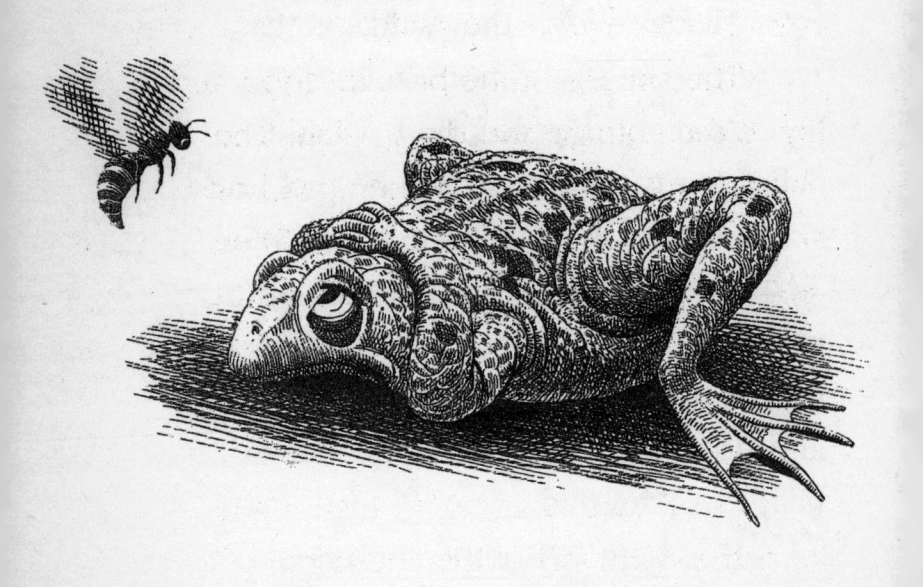

The Jewel

Just follow nature, he thought. I knew it in my bones. He laid the hard thing down and crept outside.

Through the house grew a glow of light. The woman and her children thought it was some dream of being dead.

They found the reason on the floor. It was a jewel from the head of Buff, his pain, the pain of every toad.

The shining stone brought food and joy to the cottage and dry garden. The children made for Buff a sheltered house and let him wander in and out. When daylight came he sat in his new home.

"Feeling better then," said Homberson Bomberson, flying low and loud and much too stripy.

"Yes," said Buff. With his tongue he gathered in the stripe and noise of Homberson Bomberson, and closed his mouth on him.

"Knees in, wings back," said Homberson Bomberson, too surprised to sting.

A pleasure, thought Buff, to meet someone well brought up. It's peaceful now. And tomorrow will be better still.

The Foxer

The Foxer is a hairy man who has loved to shoot and trap and dig wild creatures out. His dog Fury trots beside him, whiskered like his man.

"Beware man's dog," says badger in holt. "But Foxer will follow Fury, so beware dog's man."

They are both danger. By day they tread the farmland.

"Beware man's eye," says fox in field.

The Fox Gate

At night with searching light the Foxer walks the woods.

"Beware man's light," says vixen in earth.

Fox is not his only prey. He hunts anything.

"Beware man's gun," says hare in hay.

Fury seeks and digs with him. Fury sits by man's fire and has forgotten that free is wild.

"Beware the bag," says hog in hedge. Foxer will take all.

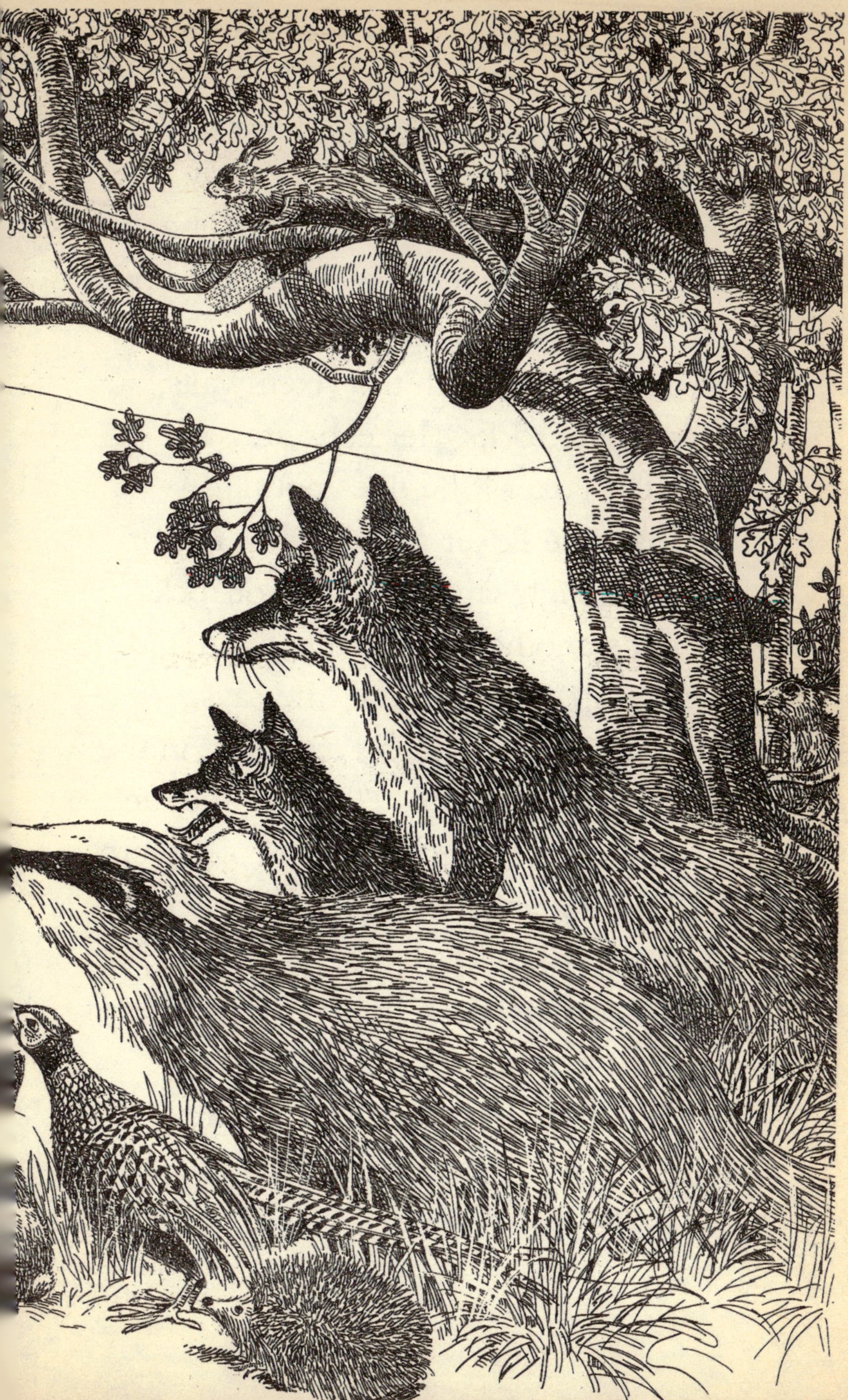

Fury snuffs each hole and every breeze. The Foxer breathes a curly pipe, and waits. He waits by night and day. Fury barks his foxer bark and finds the foxes' secret door.

Inside the earth the vixen waits, deep in the rock. Her cubs are safe from the Foxer if he does not dig.

But the Foxer will come to fox or vixen through sand, or stone, or rock. He finds another door to the earth and stops it up. "That is that," he says.

Where fox can go Fury goes, in the hollows of the rocks. Here are sudden caves; here is water tumbling cold; there are hanging spines of rock, and blind forgotten fish.

There are deep holes where floors will fall. Fury tumbles off the overhanging path into a shaft. He is not hurt beyond a bruise, but cannot climb the hard steep sides.

The Foxer waits above in open air. He fills his pipe again. Fury will soon come out, he thinks.

Vixen and fox and cubs stay silent many an hour. They hear Fury whine and call for rescue. They dare not help a thing they fear so much.

The Foxer smokes another pipe. He calls for Fury. Fury is too far lost to hear him, but others do.

"Who is trapped here?" says mole in his mine.

The Foxer walks to the earth's other door and digs it open again for Fury to come out.

"Man alone is a danger still," warns hawk on high.

The Foxer eats his meaty pie. He calls Fury for his share, but Fury is far below.

"He will die," says fox to vixen. "We dare not go near."

"We dare not go near."

Badger listens. "I do not fear, nor do I care," he says

Fury hears them stir. "You dare not come," he snarls.

"No one asked you in," says badger.

Outside there is night. The Foxer brings his searchlight, but it cannot see through rock. He listens.

Badger goes out another way. He is not lost. Fox follows him, knowing all the paths.

Fury and the Foxer call to one another, but cannot hear.

"Well, that is sad," thinks vixen. "They care, or maybe they love each other like cub and mother."

"They love to take us from the free wild," says badger.

"They ask for help," say vixen. "But I must not go near."

begins to dig. He lays aside his coat, his gun, his snares, his net and bag. He pulls out rock and opens up the ground.

He calls as he goes, but deep digging is slow. Fury sleeps, and calls to the Foxer, but begins to fear. He thinks the Foxer forgets to care.

All day the Foxer digs, the farther down the harder the work, until night comes again and he has to sleep.

He stays by the place.

He wakes and calls his dog to him, but Fury cannot come.

"Sweet dreams," says owl, safe in the moonlight.

Vixen and badger have hunted. Fox and the cubs are filled. Fury has had nothing in the dry trap.

A second whole long day the Foxer digs. He will not give up. He has cut deep. "But I fear it is a grave," he says.

Towards night Fury hears his voice.

Towards night Fury hears his voice. Fury tries to call back, but he can scarcely speak. He no longer leaps and tries to escape.

There is another night. The Foxer's fingers bleed with work. Tonight he does not dream. Then there is another day of digging. It is like moving a mountain. The Foxer thinks of gunpowder, black and loud.

"I could have told him," says mole. "But he would make me into waistcoat."

Fury now is lying still. He cannot move. Badger hears him breathe, and now and then vixen hears a wimper.

"I cannot bear the sound," she says. "What can we do?"

"Stay clear," says fox. "If man breaks through we run."

By the light of dawn the digging starts again. Fox comes home late with food for vixen, and sees the sorry man.

caught.

"Plenty for us," says vixen, and does not eat it all. The badger puts some aside. "You never know," he says.

The Foxer digs closer. Stones rattle down inside the earth and into the badger's holt. Sunshine falls into those dark houses where it never was before.

"Such pretty stuff," say the cubs, seeing sunbeams shine through dust.

Light falls on Fury. He is curled up. He calls, but he is too weak to make himself heard.

"He calls like a hungry cub," says vixen. "Must he die?"

"Many a fox has died for the Foxer," says badger. "When he has dug out the dog he will dig us out too."

"We can get away," says vixen. "But there is something I must do." Her pity will not let her rest.

"I'll walk with you to keep you

safe," says badger.

They go through the dust and sunshine and look down at Fury. Fury looks up and sees them. He opens his mouth. He cannot make a sound, and his eyes close.

"I have more than I can eat," says badger.

"I saved a little too," says vixen. They both drop down into the hole the food they brought.

At that moment the Foxer lifts a great slab of rock. He sees vixen and badger bring food to Fury. Foxer stands still and watches, wondering and amazed.

It is the first time he has considered that animals have their own lives. He sees Fury wake and eat and grow strong at once. He hears Fury speak to vixen and to badger, to say thank you.

Vixen and badger go back into the darkness.

The Foxer talks to Fury. He digs the last way down, and as he does he is ashamed that wild creatures should care for his dog, and he not care for them.

"I thought I knew," he said. "I could catch any animal, but I loved none of them. I am sorry for more than my dog."

He kisses him, and Fury licks his face. The Foxer fills in the great hole he made, and as he does he thinks.

When he has thought he throws in his searchlight, so that no one will fear his light. He drops in his gun, so the wild creatures are safe from it, and pitches in his snare and nets. He carries Fury away, who is too weak to walk.

"That time is over," he says. "I shall kill nothing more."

Fox in field and hare in hay, hog in

hedge and hawk on high, from then go on safely.

The Foxer and his Fury are their enemies no longer. Now they wait and watch and take delight in other life.

"All the same," says the badger, "that dog will get a nip if he is too friendly."

Another Story Book from Hodder Children's Books

DARK AT THE FOOT OF THE STAIRS

Eileen Moore

SPIDERS! Like them or loathe them.
Every house has got them.

But Tommy's is different.

It's bigger. Much bigger . . .

And it could be lurking just about anywhere.

It likes bananas, and frogs, and the dark at the foot of the stairs . . .

Another Story Book from Hodder Children's Books

HAMISH

W. J. Corbett

Hamish is a mountain goat.

All his friends are mountain goats.

The only trouble is - Hamish is *terrified* of climbing mountains.

Every day his friends clatter off to seek adventure in the high hills, and every day Hamish makes more and more excuses to stay behind in the comfort of his heathery bed.

Until one day, Hamish hears a cry for help - and only he can save the day . . .

HODDER'S YEAR OF STORIES
for the NATIONAL YEAR OF READING

Why not collect all twelve Story Books in *Hodder's Year of Stories*?

January	Fog Hounds, Wind Cat, Sea Mice *Joan Aiken*	0340 75274 2	£1.99 ☐
February	The Railway Cat's Secret *Phyllis Arkle*	0340 75278 5	£1.99 ☐
March	A Dog of My Own *Alan Brown*	0340 75276 9	£1.99 ☐
April	The Dragon's Child *Jenny Nimmo*	0340 75277 7	£1.99 ☐
May	Jake *Annette Butterworth*	0340 75281 5	£1.99 ☐
June	Hamish *W. J. Corbett*	0340 75275 0	£1.99 ☐
July	The Silkie *Sandra Horn*	0340 75279 3	£1.99 ☐
August	A Gift from Winklesea *Helen Cresswell*	0340 75280 7	£1.99 ☐
September	The Fox Gate *William Mayne*	0340 75282 3	£1.99 ☐
October	Dark at the Foot of the Stairs *Eileen Moore*	0340 75283 1	£1.99 ☐
November	Secret Friends *Elizabeth Laird*	0340 75284 X	£1.99 ☐
December	Milly *Pippa Goodhart*	0340 75285 8	£1.99 ☐

ORDER FORM

Please select your Year of Reading Story Books from the previous page

All Hodder Children's books are available at your local bookshop or newsagent, or can be ordered direct from the publisher. Just tick the titles you want and fill in the form below. Prices and availability subject to change without notice.

Hodder Children's Books, Cash Sales Department, Bookpoint, 39 Milton Park, Abingdon, OXON, OX14 4TD, UK. If you have a credit card you may order by telephone - (01235) 831700.

Please enclose a cheque or postal order made payable to Bookpoint Ltd to the value of the cover price and allow the following for postage and packing:
UK & BFPO - £1.00 for the first book, 50p for the second book, and 30p for each additional book ordered up to a maximum charge of £3.00.
OVERSEAS & EIRE - £2.00 for the first book, £1.00 for the second book, and 50p for each additional book.

Name..

Address ....

....

....

If you would prefer to pay by credit card, please complete:
Please debit my Visa/Access/Diner's Card/American Express (delete as applicable) card no.

Signature..

Expiry Date..